T0368458

UNBREAK-A-BLE

Ethan Mcgallion

"Zailee"

AuthorHouse™
1663 Liberty Drive
Bloomington, IN 47403
www.authorhouse.com
Phone: 833-262-8899

Because of the dynamic nature of the Internet, any web addresses or links contained in this book may have changed since publication and may no longer be valid. The views expressed in this work are solely those of the author and do not necessarily reflect the views of the publisher, and the publisher hereby disclaims any responsibility for them.

Any people depicted in stock imagery provided by Getty Images are models, and such images are being used for illustrative purposes only. Certain stock imagery © Getty Images.

This book is printed on acid-free paper.

Illustrated by Skyla Lakey
Edited by Keely Odom

ISBN: 979-8-8230-3379-4 (sc)
979-8-8230-3381-7 (hc)
979-8-8230-3380-0 (e)

Library of Congress Control Number: 2024918996

Print information available on the last page.

Published by AuthorHouse 10/16/2024

authorHOUSE

UNBREAK-A-BLE

Age: 17

gender: Female

Name: Mora Rose

Ethnicity: Puerto Rican

A long time ago in a lab in the middle of nowhere, in the middle of the forest, scientists would experiment, and study children with superpowers. These scientists would see if these kids were special enough to become the heroes of tomorrow, even if the children didn't want to be heroes. There is one specific super powered girl they believe could be useful in the future. A girl named Mora, who has the ability to create, absorb, and control energy using atoms to tap into that energy. She is a very powerful little girl, who has a lot of potential to be a great superhero. The scientists all agreed that Mora is ready to start her training as a superhero at Zand, a company that turns super humans into world famous superheroes. The scientists were talking to the CEO of Zand, Albert Zand about Mora joining Zand. There was one scientist in particular that wasn't supportive of the idea of Mora joining Zand. She knows how they treat the children there, and it's certainly not an environment that a six year old child should be in.

After talking to the other scientist, Albert made up his mind about sending Mora to join Zand. The scientist named Dr. Rose spoke to Albert about maybe reconsidering his decision, and waiting until she's a little older and more in control of her powers before handing her over to Zand. "This is not the time for waiting, this is a time for action!" Stated Albert. "She finally got her powers; she has a wonderful ability that needs to be shared with the world." "I just don't think she's ready for that life yet. She's just a kid, and I frankly don't think she is ready for the world; or maybe the world isn't ready for her." Dr. Rose said worriedly. Albert did not care for Dr. Rose's concerns, he told her his mind was already made up; and as of tomorrow she'll be transferred to Zand. Dr. Rose could not allow this to happen, she returned to her office to talk to her assistant about getting Mora out of the lab. They knew the risk they were taking by doing this, but they would rather throw away everything than become greedy monsters like them.

As everyone was leaving, Dr. Rose told her colleagues that she'll be staying a little bit to catch up on some work. Dr. Rose's assistant, Devan made sure everyone left the building, the only people in the building were the security guards. Devan gave Dr. Rose the heads up through text that the coast was clear, so Dr. Rose and Devan decided to make their move. Dr. Rose and Devan entered Mora's room, seeing her asleep in her bed. Dr. Rose had a big blanket that she wrapped Mora in, Mora awoke slightly from her slumber wondering what was going on. Dr. Rose shushed her saying that everything is ok. "It's ok sweetie. I got you." Reassured Dr. Rose. "Just go back to sleep." Said Dr. Rose. Dr. Rose carries Mora out of her room, so the three decide to make their way to the car to escape the lab. Devan pushed the button to the elevator, but when the elevator doors opened, trouble appeared on the other side. Albert Zand and a group of security guards were prepared for what Dr. Rose had planned; and decided to surprise them.

"Don't you just love high tech security?" Albert asked rhetorically. The guards surrounded the three escapees with guns loaded and ready to fire. While standing with arms in the air, Devan whispers to Dr. Rose. "I'm about to do something; and when I do run for the elevator...", "Hey! No talking!" Shouted a guard. Dr. Rose was nervous because she did not know what was about to happen. Devan looked at the guard who silenced him; and said, "You must think you're a real badass with that gun in your hand.", "I said no talking!" The guard shouted once more. "Let's see how tough you are without it!" Devan threatened the guard, while throwing a punch to the guard's face." Come on! Let's see what you mother fuckers are really made of!" exclaimed Devan. Dr. Rose went with the plan; and went for the elevator to head up to the elevator. While the elevator doors slowly closed, Dr. Rose saw her friend was being beaten; and held by his arms. Albert Zand pulled a gun out of his suit pocket, aimed; and shot Devan right through his head.

A tear dropped from Dr. Rose's left eye as she heard the gunshot that ended her friend's life. She wiped the tear from her cheek and decided to put on a brave face; and continue the mission. The elevator took her and Mora to the garage so that they could make their escape. Dr. Rose got to her car, placed Mora gently in the back seat of the car; and then started her car. As Dr. Rose was driving towards the exit, the guards tried to block her exit by placing an access board in front of her. So Dr. Rose put the pedal to the metal and broke the access board, exiting out of the facility. Dr. Rose succeeded in escaping the lab, saving Mora from a life of torture. While Dr. Rose knew she couldn't go back to her home, knowing Zand would be there to take Mora away from her. Dr. Rose decides to go to Hillsview, a city miles away from Zand; and a safe place to raise Mora. She must make sure no one knows that she is a superhuman; and must keep her powers a secret from the world.

Twelve years later, we see Mora at the age close to adulthood. She is seventeen, Mora and Dr. Rose have lived in a house in the city of Hillsview for a long time. We see sweet, young, Mora asleep in her bed as the sunlight enters her room through her window. Her room is pink, with white LED lights surrounding each corner of her roof. She has a small walk-in closet, stuffed animals surrounding her window, and an iPhone with a white cat phone case. Speaking of her phone, her phone wakes Mora up with an alarm. She wakes up, changing out of her nighttime attire; and dressing for the day. We see Dr. Rose coming downstairs putting on her lab coat, for she worked as a doctor in a local hospital. She yelled for Mora, telling her that she must get ready for school, she then sees Mora cooking eggs on the stove. "Scrambled or fried?" Mora asked with a smile. "What do you think?" Dr. Rose answered with a smile. "Scrambled it is." Said Mora. Dr. Rose sits down at the kitchen table as Mora cooked breakfast.

"You know I could've made breakfast this morning." Said Dr. Rose. "I know I just wanted to do something nice for my mom." Said Mora. Dr. Rose maybe just another character to us, but to Mora she was a mother. This is how she earned the role as Mora's mom. Years ago, when Dr. Rose and Mora moved into their present home, Dr. Rose needed to talk to Mora about the living situation. "This is our new home now, but we need to set up some ground rules." Announced Dr. Rose. "When we're inside and no one is around you are free to use your gifts. No one can ever see you using your powers, nor can you show anyone your powers. Can you do that for me?" asked Dr. Rose. "Can I call you mom?" Mora answered with a question. A tear drop of joy fell from Dr. Rose's left eye. "Yes." Answered Dr. Rose. "Then yes." Mora answering the first request. Dr. Rose opened her arms giving a tight, warm, hug to Mora. On that day their love, bond, and relationship finally rose. That is how Dr. Rose got her new name as Mom.

Now back to the present, we see Mora making a plate of scrambled eggs for her and her mother. Mora grabs two pieces of toast out of the toaster and places one toast on each plate. The TV was on, a news report came on about the superhero team, the United, defeating the super villain team known as the Wicked. The United is a group of Earth's greatest heroes united as one hence the name the United. The villains of the Wicked were Reflex, Goliath, Brain Storm, Korcus, Jellyfish, and their leader, Doctor Seize. Reflex was a villain who was a master of martial arts; and a master of knowing someone's next move. His power is to predict his enemies next move, so that he can dodge it. His power works by flashes of the future revealed to him in the next second. Goliath is a villain who has the power to grow into the size of a giant. Brain Storm is a villain who has telepathic and telekinetic abilities. Korcus is an alien warrior that is part of the Wicked, and down for the cause of evil. A big, strong, red, alien with muscles the size of cars. He also carried a mallet with spikes on it. Jellyfish was the female member of the group, her powers were odd to some but were quite useful. She had jellyfish tentacles to grab things, or even shock people. Now for the leader Doctor Seize, he formed the group to destroy the United. Doctor Seize was a scientist who created a powerful suit of armor, powerful enough to take on the United.

The United was a team of Earth's greatest heroes, and the planet's number one best superhero team. Valiant is the leader of the United, he is one of the most powerful heroes on the planet. He can fly, has super strength, heat vision, ice breath, and he is invulnerable. Moonlight is the vigilante in the group, not much is known about him. He doesn't have any confirmed superpowers; he is a very mysterious character. All we know about him is he is a master of martial arts and is a great fighter to the team.

Next we have three members named Warrior Woman, Road Runner, and Green Guardian, who are super humans. Not every superhero is a superhuman, some of them get their powers from somewhere else, like Valiant, even though he looks human, he is actually an alien. He came to Earth as a baby in a space pod, he was found by Zand and the scientists who found him. He gained his powers from the Earth's atmosphere opening his alien genes to reveal his powers. Now super humans on the other hand are humans inherited with a gene that gives them powers, and that gene can be activated in many ways, like through birth, puberty, traumatic situations, or even exposure to radiation. Super humans have existed on Earth for millennia and we don't really know who is a superhuman until one pops up. There have been dozens of controversial battles between humans and super humans for a long time.

The United is lucky to have three super humans on their team, plus they want to teach humans that super humans are not a threat. Warrior Woman is the female member of the team, her superhuman powers consist of the angelic wings on her back. Her superhuman genes kicked in when she got her first period, when she was twelve, and wings grew out of her back. Today she uses her wings to travel to wherever crime lies. She dresses like an angel in armor with a sword and a shield, to be an inspiration to little girls everywhere to show them that women can be warriors too. Road Runner is a superhuman with the ability to run faster than the speed of light. He calls himself Road Runner because he thinks of himself as the bird who runs really fast. The next member is a superhuman named Green Guardian, who has the ability to communicate with plant life; and he uses that ability to use plants to help him fight evil. The last hero on the team is the Uranian, an alien from the planet Uranus. He came to Earth to defend the planet, very similar to Valiant.

These are our heroes, Earth's greatest heroes. Mora looked up to the United because she is a person who wants to use her powers to protect the world. She always wanted to be a superhero, plus one day be a member of the United. She knows her mother would never allow it though, because she doesn't want anyone to think that she is special. Not in a shameful way, but in a protective way. Dr. Rose knew Mora's true feelings, but she thought maybe she could change her feelings. "So, I heard homecoming is coming in a couple of weeks. Has anyone asked you out to the dance, or have you asked anyone?" asked Dr. Rose. "I thought I wasn't supposed to be socializing?" Mora answered with a question. "I never said that I said...", "Get good grades and keep my head on the low." said Mora. "That's not fair, Mora." replied Dr. Rose. "Just saying, that's how it is." said Mora. Dr. Rose sighed with exhaustion after Mora's argumentative behavior. "I thought this was going to be a good morning." gaslighted Dr. Rose.

Mora felt bad for making her mother's morning difficult, which we all knew wasn't Mora's fault. Her mother just didn't want to properly communicate, she decided to turn her stress over to her daughter to make her feel bad. So, after the gaslight Mora said she needed to get to school. So she grabbed her backpack and opened the door to head out the sidewalk to get to school. Before she left, Dr. Rose told Mora, "I love you, Mora!" That comment made her forget about the gaslight, it felt good to hear her mom say those words. She smiled and said, "I love you too, mom!" Mora walked to the bus stop; we see a young man waving at her. He had dark brown hair, a funny smile, and wore a black and white shirt with an orange flannel over it. "Hey girl!" greeted the young man. "What's up boy?!" Mora greeted back to the young man. The young man was named Jessie, he was Mora's best, and only friend. "So, what's the news my friend, how was your weekend?" asked Jessie, as they both walked on the school bus. "Boring just watched half of the third season of Diary of A Teenage Vampire, and made fanfic about Moonlight and Valiant." answered Mora.

"What is up with you watching early two thousands tv show? Also, why Valiant and Moonlight?" asked Jessie. "I like shows from back then, they were so much better. The reason for the fanfiction is because the thought of Valiant bending Moonlight over and...", "Nope! Let's keep it PG please." Jessie said while covering his ears with his fingers. "Ok, the thought of Valiant and Moonlight being an item is very attractive." said Mora. "What about you?" asked Mora. "Did my paper route which I do every morning, played video games; and spent time with my main dog, RC." answered Jessie. As the school bus drove past many streets...she began seeing what looked like atoms, electrons, protons, and neutrons. It was crazy, it was like seeing space or something. She saw one atom that was glowing pink, on and off. Mora was amazed at what she was seeing, she wanted to touch it. She slowly reaches out to the Atom, a pink electric energy bounced from her fingertips to the atom. She took her hand back due to the unusual reaction, but she couldn't help but try to touch the atom. She decides to try again

She puts her hand back in the air, pink electric like energy began conducting with the atom. As she was close to touch the atom she was interrupted by a disturbed voice, "What do you think you're doing?!" Mora wakes up from the illusion of atoms, back to reality. Mora didn't know but her hand was close to the shoulder of Hope Hartley. The most popular girl in Hillsview High. Mora was shocked at what she unknowingly was going to do. After Hope left, Mora couldn't stop thinking about the incredible things she saw. "Are you ok?" asked Jessie. "Yeah, I'm cool." Mora answered with uncertainty. "Is that like a girl hormone thing?" asked Jessie. "No." answered Mora. As Mora and Jessie wet riding the bus, Mora wondered if this was a new ability that she unlocked. Now this wasn't the first time she has seen things like atoms, electrons, and other things. What made it different was the pink energy; and the connection she had with it.

Meanwhile at Mark City, a meteor shower was headed towards the city thankfully Valiant, and Warrior Woman appeared to save the day. Valiant using his super punches; and heat vision to destroy the meteors. Warrior Woman using her uncanny sword to slice through the meteors. Eventually all the meteors were destroyed, the people of Mark City cheered for the heroes for saving them from no longer existing. The two heroes looked at each other eye to eye and smiled with love. They fly to each other, getting closer, and closer. "You were absolutely amazing." complimented Warrior Woman. "So were you." replied Valiant. Valiant takes Warrior Woman by her lower back; and brings her closer to him. Leans in for a kiss, but before the two love birds can share their kiss both of their United wrist watches begin to go off. An alert from Mount United, the Uranian sounded the alarm as it clearly indicates on the watch. Valiant used his watch to call Moonlight." Moonlight, did you get the alert?" asked Valiant. "Yes." answered Moonlight.

"Ok I'm sending Road Runner to pick you, and Green Guardians up." said Valiant. Warrior Woman contacts Road Runner to pick up Moonlight, and Green Guardian. Road Runner uses his super speed to pick up both Moonlight and Green Guardian, rushing the two heroes to Mount United. Green Guardian vomits after they stopped at the entrance of Mount United. "Looks like GG still isn't use to super speed travel." said Moonlight. Valiant and Warrior Woman appear from the sky, coming down to join their friends. Moonlight opens the door; the team enters inside their lair. Valiant looks above and sees the Uranian quietly sitting in the chair facing the supercomputer with the alarm still going off. "Uranian!" Valiant exclaimed as he flew to his friend. He turned the chair around and saw both of the Uranian's eyes burned to a crisp, shocking Valiant seeing his friend dead. "Who did this?!" Moonlight asked with rage. All of the sudden a mysterious figure in a green cloak appears with yellow eyes, the cloak's shade was so dark it covered the figure's face making it hard to see what his face really looked like. The team knew that he was a threat, and figured he was the one who killed their friend

Green Guardian used his vine grapplers from his wrist to attack the green cloaked figure. "You'll pay for what you've done!" screamed Green Guardian. The green cloaked figure dodged Green Guardian's attack; he dodged it by running fast as if he had the same speed as Road Runner somehow. He used his speed to grab Green Guardian by the neck part of Green Guardian's skeleton tearing his own skeleton from his own body. "NO!" cried Warrior Woman. Moonlight came to the scene and began fighting the cloaked figure, eventually got the figure into a headlock." Who are you?! What do you want with us?!" Moonlight asked confrontationally. The figure took a knife stabbing Moonlight in the stomach to break free from Moonlight's headlock. Moonlight dropped to his knees as his stomach slowly bled, the cloaked figure then chopped Moonlight's head clean off his body by doing a side karate chop slicing his head off his body as if it was a watermelon. Valiant flew over to the figure trying to catch him, but the figure used his super speed again to run from being caught by Valiant.

Road Runner began chasing the cloaked figure to see if he could catch up. Road Runner eventually caught up with him and shoved him to the wall. He tries grabbing the figure's cloak to see if he can see who this psycho really is but the cloaked figure grabbed Road Runner's hand before it could touch his hood. The figure broke his arm by jerking his arm up dislocating both bones in the elbow area of his left arm, with both bones sticking outside of his arm. Road Runner screamed in pain as Warrior Woman jumped in the air with her sword ready to attack the cloaked figure. He uses Road Runner as shield to protect himself from Warrior Woman's sword attack, resulting in Road Runner being sliced in half by his teammate. Warrior Woman is then traumatized by what she unintentionally just did, terrified at seeing the blood of her friend all over her face. The cloaked figure then picks Warrior Woman by the neck trying to choke her, but she uses her combat skills to kick herself off him. Valiant then arrives using his ice breath to contain the foe, which it did for about 10 seconds.

The cloaked figure broke out with wings like Warrior Woman. This threat must have the same powers as all the United combined. Suddenly the cloaked figure had a dust of yellow radiation in his hands and blew it out of his hands towards Valiant's direction. It turns out the radiation is actually Zimpherion, a radiation that weakens Valiant and even causes his powers to shut down. Valiant felt weak after being covered in the radioactive, dusty, substance. He began coughing; and even began to feel dizzy. It was up to Warrior Woman to save herself; and to save Valiant from their own deaths. Warrior Woman fought the cloaked figure using her combat skills; and her sword to fight for her life. The cloaked figure kicked Warrior Woman in the face knocking her down, while she was down the cloaked figure turned her around; and ripped the wings right out of her back. Warrior Woman screamed in pain, and agony as her wings were roughly ripped from her back.

Warrior Woman tries to crawl away from the cloaked figure while in pain, but the cloaked figure ends the defenseless hero by taking her own sword and stabbing her through the back to the outside of her stomach, causing a slow, and painful death for the superhero as she slowly dies in her own pool of blood. The cloaked figure then turns his attention to Valiant, seeing him on the ground weak and powerless. The cloaked figure grabbed Valiant by his neck choking him with his left arm. "Justice will prevail." Valiant whispered as he slowly began to see the light of the afterlife flash before his eyes. There the most powerful man; and the most powerful superhero team in the entire universe was killed by the cloaked figure. The cloaked figure slowly walked away from the scene, before he walked out of the building, he looked at all the heroes he just killed and said, "Justice will prevail..." Scoffed the cloaked figure. "What a bunch of bullshit." mocked the cloaked figure as he exited the building.

Meanwhile at Hillsview High, we see our main character, Mora, walking down the hall to the women's restroom, where she sees two girls bullying another. "Let go of me!" demanded the bullied girl. "Or what you going to flash me with your three inch **** huh? You going to flash me you little pervert?!" Insulted the female bully. "I'm not a pervert!" the bullied girl explained with anger." The female bully slapped the bullied girl in the face, causing a purple bruise to form in her left cheek. "Yes, you are! You probably use this transformer business to get away with being a pervert and have a reason to look at us while we pee!" Insulted the female bully. "It's pronounced trans...", before the bullied girl could finish, she was slapped again except this time on the right cheek of her face. "Don't interrupt me while I'm talking pervert!" insulted the female bully. "Hey!" shouted Mora. "Stop harassing her!" shouted Mora. "Oh yeah..." the female bully said as she walked to Mora. "What are you going to do about it?" asked the female bully.

Mora looked at the female bully's eye with red fury! She balled up her fist and took a punch to her face. "Ow! What the fuck?!" exclaimed the female bully. "You asked what I was going to do about it, well that's what I was going to do." explained Mora. She looked at the other female bully who was holding the captive bullied girl and asked, "You want some too?", "Nah, I'm good." answered the other female bully while running away cowardly. "Fuck this I'm out!" said the punched, female, bully as she left the scene. Mora helped the bullied girl up. "Are you ok?" asked Mora. "I'm fine, it's not like I'm not used to things like this." answered the bully girl. "My name is Mora." Introduced Mora. "What's yours? asked Mora. Before the bullied girl could say anything, a loud alert went off on their phones. Not just them, but everyone's phone had loud alert notifications popping up on their phone, it looked like something about the United.

Mora and everyone across the world clicked on the notification; and it showed a live news broadcast indicating that the United have been murdered. The people of this world's mouths dropped, their eyes wide open, tears falling from the bottom of their eyes, and sighing of depression. Now the world is left without their greatest heroes to protect them, sure there were other heroes out there, they just don't compare to the United, because they were truly Earth's greatest heroes. Now they're gone, and now the world stands in uncertainty of the safety of the world. Mora couldn't believe this; this was the worst news she ever heard. It was her dream to fight alongside the United, but now her dream has been crushed by the hardness of reality. Many heroes sent their condolences like the Fabulouses, the Monster Society, the Mysticals, and the Youth of Tomorrow, telling the world how missed the United will be. A funeral service would be held tomorrow by Zand industries, asking everyone who loved the United to come for the service.

The next day, the funeral service for the United commenced. Mora was watching the live broadcast of the funeral service on her TV in her room, she asked her mother if they could attend the service, but she said no. So, Mora had to watch the service in the comfort of her own home. Many sad faces on the screen, Albert Zand took the stage and made a speech about how even though the United are gone. "Even in our darkest hours we must continue to try to search for that light at the end of the other side. Just because the United are gone, doesn't mean that the hope we've within us is gone too." said Albert Zand. Suddenly something that Albert Zand stuck with Mora as she listened to his speech. He said, "Remember anyone can become a hero!" That stuck with Mora, because she always felt like it was her destiny to become a superhero; and save the world from evil. Atoms ignited in her eyes giving her an awakening, a flower within her that just needed to be blossomed to life. She knew her mother would never approve of her being a superhero, so she must keep it in secret but first she must better control her abilities.

After the funeral service was over, Mora headed to her backyard in her house to master her abilities. She knew she could fly, and she has tough skin. What she really wanted to master was that atom touching thing that happened to her on the bus, because she believed she was seeing something that could be useful to her. She tries taking a deep breath and tries to make the particles appear in mid-air like last time but no luck. She tried several times to bring it back, she began to become agitated. Her anger overcame her, causing her eyes to glow pink and she threw her hands down in anger. Suddenly it all came back to her, all the particles were there before her. She realized how to now summon this ability, by really, really wanting it. If she wants it so badly, she must want it so badly in order for it to appear. She put her hands in the air feeling one atom, connecting to all atoms around her giving her a sense of euphoria. The power of all the atoms crawling all through her body, giving her a nice feeling because of all the power surging through her.

Something else happened, she began to see something new. Everything was black, and pink glowing around her at the same time. It was strange, but she felt connected to everything. Like she could change anything...she looked at the tree in her back yard, suddenly the whole tree turned from being made of wood to be made of glass. This surprises Mora because she believes it was her that made this happen; she looked around her surroundings to see if anyone else saw what she did. So far, the coast was clear, no witnesses to witness the weird event. She tries using her powers to change it back, which she successfully does. She smiles, as she knows she is getting better control over her powers. She decided to try something out just to make sure she has this whole thing down. She looked to the grass that she was standing on, she used her powers to change the color of it turning it pink. Then changed it from pink to blue, then blue to purple, and then purple back to green. She could not believe her eyes, she had the power to change anything she wanted to change.

Now that Mora has successfully mastered her abilities, now she must create a disguise so that no one can see who she really is. So, she went up to her room took some clothes to see if she could come up with an outfit. By the end all she could come up with is a pink sweatshirt, a pink mask made out of foam, and blue jeans. She didn't like the results because she wanted to look like a superhero, not an Old Navy mannequin. So, she used her newfound powers to want the suit, that she wants. In the span of ten whole seconds the clothes on her body turned into an instant superhero suit of her design. Mora was amazed how the suit looked, looking exactly like she imagined in her mind. So now with her mastered powers, and her own superhero suit she was ready to save the world! She used her powers to open her window, flying out of her room and into the night air. For the first time ever, she finally felt free, like her full authentic self.

She entered the city of Hillsview with optimism that there would be crime to happen. Unfortunately, she realized that crime fighting is not as sudden as she thought it would be. She sat on the ledge of an apartment building for hours, and hours waiting for the opportunity to arise. From dying of boredom, she passed the time by eating gas station snacks, watching TikTok, and even whistling, trying to catch a tune. Suddenly she hears a loud bang! She decides to fly over and investigate the loud sound, it came from an abandoned warehouse where she heard noises that sounded like a fight. She used her hands like binoculars to see inside the building to see what the commotion is about. It appears to be a fight between a hero and a villain, Mora uses her abilities to create a literal door to the building to help the hero. The villain had sharp claws like a sabretooth tiger trying to scratch the hero, as Mora was observing the fight between the hero and villain, she noticed that the hero looked very familiar.

The hero had a moon symbol attached to his cloak, sort of like Moonlight. Suddenly the villain scratched Moonlight in the right side of his face causing half of his cheek to be seen, thank God he didn't cut further into his mask, or his secret identity would've been revealed. The villain with the claws was getting ready to give the hero another slice, Mora had to do something and fast! "Nighty night, Moonlight! Ha ha ha!" cackled the villain as he was ready to end Moonlight's life. Mora used her powers to create a blast that blasts the villain out of the building and into the streets, where he lands slam shut into a dumpster. Moonlight was surprised at what happened, Mora flew over to Moonlight's safety. "You're Moonlight?" asked Mora. "If you mean the new one, then yes." answered Moonlight. "I don't understand. Moonlight is dead." Mora said with confusion. "Look kid I don't have time to explain all of this, you need to go and play superhero someplace else, this is my territory." said Moonlight.

"Who was that?" asked Mora. "That was the Maniac, one of the most deviant villains in this city." answered Moonlight. "I must go, the police will come any second now." said Moonlight. Moonlight used his grapple wrist band to zip line his way out of the scene. "Wait!..." yelled Mora as he disappeared from the scene. Mora was so confused; how could Moonlight be alive if he was murdered a day ago? Mora heard police sirens coming, so she decides to leave them a surprise. The cops arrived at the alleyway where the Maniac was and tied him up using a light pole to hold him for the cops. The cops were totally shocked at what they saw, mouths dropped bigger than the mouth of a hippopotamus. "Now who did this?" asked one of the cops. Mora was soaring through the night sky, feeling a sense of greatness due to her heroic act. This feeling felt right, it felt astonishing, and so good! She sneaks back to her house through her window, changing her heroes clothes to pajamas. Then going to bed to slumber with a smile on her face.

The next day, Dr. Rose made toast for breakfast. Mora used her flying powers to zoom her way to the kitchen. "How did you sleep?" asked Dr. Rose. "I slept fine." answered Mora. The TV was showing a news report on the Maniac, talking about how he was captured by an unknown hero. So now the media is wondering who was this mysterious hero; and when will we get to see this hero? Mora smiled as people were curious about who she is; and when she would actually show up to the public as their hero. This made Mora feel important, and special. Mora looked at the time on her phone, realizing that her bus would be here at any moment. She zooms back to her room to grab her backpack, kisses her mother on the cheek, telling her that she loves her, and telling her bye. She ran to the bus stop, she could've zoomed her way there, but she didn't want anyone to see her powers. She misses the bus, but luckily for her she used her powers to fly herself to school.

As Jessie gets off the bus at Hillsview High, he sees Mora at the entrance of the school. "What's up boy?!" greeted Mora. Jessie was surprised to see her at school before him, he thought she would be late for school since she was late for the bus. "How did you get here?" asked Jessie. Mora had to come up with a lie and fast... "I took an Uber." fibbed Mora. "Uber? Since when did you start taking Ubers?" asked Jessie. "Since now." answered Mora. After Jessie was done asking questions, he and his best friend walked down the halls to their class. As they were walking down the halls, Mora saw the girl she helped in the bathroom the other day. Mora greets her with a hey, but the little girl clenched onto her jacket and looked away. Mora was weirded out by her face; she looked like she didn't want to be seen by her. "You know that girl?" asked

Jessie. "Yeah, a couple of girls were picking on her in the restroom the other day. I stopped them from beating her...I don't understand why she just hid from me?" Mora answered with confusion.

"Why is she hiding from you?" asked Jessie. "I don't know." answered Mora. The two friends make it to their first class, which is science class. Their teacher, Mr. Finkleman enters wishing everyone a good morning, getting ready with the lesson at hand. He announces an assignment will be due for the class tomorrow, this project will be a double team assignment. The project is finding out something interesting about a subject, and an hypothesis on what that interesting thing is. Mora and Jessie looked at each other with their fingers crossed hoping the two of them would be put together for the assignment. The teacher announces names of people partnering up for their own projects. Unfortunately, Jessie was paired up with a guy named Gus in class, better known as the school geek. Mr. Finkleman named Mora's partner by the end of the calling; Mora's partner would be none other than Hope Hartley. "What?!" shouted both Mora and Hope at the same time.

"Mr. Finkleman, can I please have another partner I don't think I'm exactly comfortable with working with freaks?!" begged Hope. "You're assigned with the partner that I assigned you with, case closed." said Mr. Finkleman. Mora makes a gun shape on her right hand, pretending to blow her brains out. The reason why is because she is totally not excited to partner with Hope Hartley, due to her thinking that Mora is a freak. She is afraid of going to her house, or her going to Mora's house. The possibilities of how this can go is stressful. She looks over to Jessie with panic and says, "Help me!" with no voice coming out of her mouth. All of the sudden an alarm goes off; a school announcement is made that there is a super villain among school grounds, and everyone needs to evacuate the school immediately. Mora's hopelessness all of the sudden turned to hope again, for this meant that she could become her heroic self again.

Everybody exited out of their classrooms, going outside of the school. Mora ran to the bathroom to change into her superhero suit. She goes into a stall, locks the door; and uses her powers to change her clothes into her superhero suit to turn into her superhero persona. She walks out of the bathroom ready for action. She hears a commotion in a classroom of ninth graders. She sees a big villain with one big eye talking to the police over the phone. "Make one bad movie and these brats are fried, you got that?! threatened the villain. The villain destroyed the phone with his big right hand, smashing it into pieces. Mora enters the classroom to do what all superheroes do best! "Hey asshole." said Mora. "Why don't you pick on someone your own size?" asked Mora. "Girl, do you know who I am?!" the villain asked in offense. "No." answered Mora. "I'm the Blaster!" introduced the Blaster. "The Blaster? That is the dumbest villain name I've ever heard." replied Mora. "No, it's not! It's totally cool!" exclaimed the Blaster.

"Look buddy, just let the ninth graders go; and no villain has to get hurt." said Mora. "Or else what pip squeak?" asked the Blaster. "You really want to find out?" Mora answered with her eyes glowing pink. The Blaster's one eye turned red as he said, "Yeah I do." Mora flew towards the Blaster, the Blaster used the power of his one eye to blast her with his laser eye but he missed. She punches him in the face knocking him to the ground. Mora tells the kids to get out of the school and join everyone else outside. Suddenly the Blaster blasts her with a green laser from his eye, blasting her out of the classroom, and into the hallway. Mora gets up all dizzy and unable to focus. "What the hell?" Mora asked with confusion as she tried getting up without falling again. "I see you've experienced my dizzy beam, don't worry it only last for a minute." said the Blaster. As she was out of focus, the Blaster uses this time to physically beat her. He hit her with all types of rays, punches, and kicks to the stomach knocking her all over the place.

After the effects of the dizzy beam wore off, Mora was back throwing punches and kicks to the Blaster. Suddenly the Blaster blasts her with a purple beam, causing her body to become paralyzed. Mora couldn't move a muscle; she was completely paralyzed. "It's a good thing I used my paralyzing beam, now I can finish you off!" exclaimed the Blaster. The Blaster then began smashing his foot on her back several times causing blood to come from her nose, a bruise on her face, and even a black eye. The Blaster decides to finish her off by hitting her with his red laser beam, so he did blasting her chest. She felt the pain of the laser, the villain smiled as he knew he was going to win this battle. All of the sudden, a boomerang shaped like a bird hits his eye, causing his eyes to stop blasting; and to start bleeding. The Blaster screamed in pain as he covered his eye, because of all the blood that was spilling. We see a hero in what seems a blue bird costume, he was the one who threw the boomerang.

The figure in the blue bird superhero suit asks Mora if she is ok, she couldn't answer due to her being paralyzed. After a missed blast by the Blaster, the attention of the blue bird hero was back to the villain. As the blue bird hero was fighting the Blaster, Mora looked at her chest seeing not a scratch is made. She came to the realization that she may have just discovered a new power within herself, the power of invulnerability. The blue bird hero pulls out a gun with ropes that would strap on to the Blaster holding him. Mora's paralyzation eventually wore off, so she got up and went over to talk to the blue bird costume. "Hey sorry for not answering you before, but I just wanted to say that was really cool what you just did!" Mora said with excitement. "Thanks." replied the blue bird hero. "What's your name?" asked Mora. "Blue Bird." answered Blue Bird. "Did you make those gadgets yourself?" asked Mora. "Something like that." answered Blue Bird.

Before Mora could ask another question, two other costumes heroes randomly appeared on the scene. The two heroes were females, one had a suit that looked like a red tiger. The other one had a suit that was green and white; and had a mask that covered her eyes. "Who's ready to get fucked..." yelled the red tiger female superhero, but paused once she sees that the villain was already apprehended. "Up?" Awkwardly said the red tiger female superhero. "Rubber Girl and Scarlet Tiger, what are you guys doing here?" asked Blue Bird. "Same as you, came to kick names and take ass!" answered the Scarlet Tiger. "It's take names and kick ass." corrected Rubber Girl. "Oh right... Kick names and kick ass!" said Scarlet Tiger. Rubber Girl placed her hand over her face due to the ridiculousness of what Scarlet Tiger just said. "You guys know each other?" asked Mora. "Yeah, we've ran into each other once or twice before." answered Blue Bird. All of the sudden the cops bust into the school, seeing the Blaster apprehended by the four heroes.

The four heroes bring the villain outside the school to show everyone their tremendous victory! Everyone cheers on for Mora, Blue Bird, Rubber Girl, and the Scarlet Tiger. The four heroes waved, thanking the people for their cheering. Mora felt like a true superhero at that moment! Suddenly, we see a limo pull up and the person to come out of the car is Albert Zand.

Albert Zand congratulates the heroes for them saving their school. He talks to them about joining Zand if they are interested, he hands them all business cards to give them his contact info. Mora was so excited because this meant that her dreams of becoming a world famous superhero could come true. Albert Zand put his hand on Mora's left shoulder saying, "I believe you can be the next greatest hero!" He waves bye to the heroes, telling them before he goes that he hopes to hear from them soon.

As Albert Zand left, the three heroes besides Mora leave the scene. Mora decides to leave the scene herself, so she goes around the school where no one can see the hero and changes back to her secret identity as Mora. She walks around, she sees Jessie running to Mora. "Mora! Where were you?! There was a super villain at our school I was worried about you!" worried Jessie. "I know I just hid in the janitors closet." explained Mora. "What?! Why?!" asked Jessie. "I don't know I panicked and just hid." answered Mora Jessie hugs Mora tightly, thanking God that Mora was alive. "I thought I lost you." said Jessie as a tear from his eye left his left eye. "It's ok. I'm ok, really I am." assured Mora. Jessie used his finger to push a string of hair from Mora's face, causing an attractive tension between him and Mora. "I just don't want anything bad to happen to you." said Jessie. After all of that, the school decided to let the kids go out early due to the super villain attack today to just process and cope with what just happened.

The school buses arrive to take the kids home. Mora thought of Albert Zand's offer. She thought to herself, this could be the offer of a lifetime. Mora and Jessie get on the bus to sit at her usual stop, but then we see Mora all the way in the back of the bus, on the right side. "What do you think you're doing?" Hope asked rudely. "About to sit down." answered Mora. "No, we've an assignment due tonight and I don't know where you live. So, park your ass right next to me, so I know when to get off with you." said Hope. As Mora was moving her stuff to Hope's seat, Jessie wishes Mora luck for the terror she's about to endure with Hope. But even with the horrible fate she is bound to experience with Hope, she couldn't help but smile at what a terrific job she done today. Meanwhile we see what appears to be a bird, but it's actually a robot with a security camera that's disguised as a bird used to spy on Mora. We see footage of Mora changing back to herself on recorded footage outside of her school in the back of school.

The video footage was played in a security room at a secret lab run by none other than Zand. Albert Zand was even watching the footage with the scientists. "That's Mora!" exclaimed Albert. "Yes sir, it is." replied one of the scientists. "Mora belongs here, we must bring her here." said Albert. "Let's give her a couple of days, and if she refuses...Then we'll take her; and anyone who dares to step in our way!" threatened Albert. Meanwhile, we travel back to Mora. Where we see her and Hope get off at her house, before Mora gets off the bus she waves bye to her friend Jessie. Mora and her destroyer head to Mora's house, when Mora enters, she is hugged by her mother. "I heard what happened, are you ok?" asked Dr. Rose. "We're fine, Mom, really." answered Mora. Dr. Rose sees Mora's company, Hope. "Oh, who is this?" asked Dr. Rose. "This is Hope." answered Mora. "Is she a friend of yours?" asked Dr. Rose. "Partner for a school project." answered Hope.

An awkward silence broke between the three females, for it was clear that Hope is only concerned about the project and not a possible friendship with Mora. "Are you going to show me your room?" asked Hope. "Um...Yes, right this way." answered Mora. Mora and Hope head up the stairs to Mora's room. When they entered the room, Hope examined every inch of the room. "Cool room...if I wanted a ten year old sleepover." mocked Hope. "Yeah, I've been meaning to change this room for a while now." lied Mora. Hope giggled as she knew that was a lie, but that didn't matter for they both had a project that was due tomorrow. "Ok, we need to figure out what is an interesting scientific subject; and what makes it interesting." said Hope. The two thought for a minute or two, until an idea popped into Mora's head. She has discovered so much about atoms, electrons, and protons why not do something on that, but of what exactly?

"What about something involving atoms?" suggested Mora. "Keep talking." Hope said with interest. "There's so many cool things about atoms we can use for our projects!" exclaimed Mora. "Like what?" asked Hope. "Like...like...How atoms are important to us, and the universe. Without atoms the entire universe, including ourselves, would collapse into a black hole of nothingness. It would be like a big bang that would end everything around us. All chemical bonds would collapse, not to mention the disintegration of all solid and liquid materials. Because atoms are the fundamental blocks of matter which literally creates all of existence!" Mora explained with excitement. She then stops to see Hope with a pause, Mora thought there was going to be now a bigger awkward silence. Like way worse than the one downstairs, but instead Hope smiles and says, "Cool." Mora sighed with relief that she didn't freak her out. "We can use that for our project, we'll call it the What If of Doom." said Hope. "That's perfect!" shouted Mora.

After the girls decided what their project would be on, they begin thinking of ways how they would present this to the class. They were thinking about making a cardboard presentation with some pictures of space, atoms, elements, and percentages for their cardboard presentation. As they were working, Mora couldn't help to notice the beauty of the person she was working with. Hope twirled her hair with her left index finger, just twirling it; and twisting it as she talked. For Mora it seemed like space appeared again with atoms, electrons, and neutrons everywhere. In the center of it was Hope, it's like she was part of Mora's world almost. We know that she is just doing her assignment project, but Mora couldn't help but to want to just cuddle right next to her; and set her head on the right side of her shoulder. A song by Awfultune called "Lovesick" even began playing at this moment, a song that is Mora's favorite and a song whenever she thinks about love. All of the sudden, the lovely moment stopped when Hope asked her a question.

"Did you get that?" asked Hope, "Huh? Get what?" asked Mora. Hope rolled her eyes as she tried to explain all over again about Mora emailing over the pictures of the particles to Hope so that she can print them out at her house, because Hope is the only one with a printer at her house. "Ok, got it." confirmed Mora. There was a moment they both looked at each other eye to eye, Mora was drawn closer to Hope having this feeling of wanting to touch her lips with hers. Before anything could happen, Hope turned away. "Well, this wasn't a total waste of time after all I guess I'll see you for our presentation for class tomorrow." said Hope. "Yeah totally, see you tomorrow." replied Mora. As Hope left Mora's room, Mora dropped to her bed putting her hand over her heart for she felt an exciting feeling that made her feel a warmth and joy. Mora felt as if she awoken a feeling that she had never awakened before. She has always liked guys, but a girl, that's a new one for her.

After that warm feeling ended, she walked down to the kitchen to get a snack. Out of nowhere, Dr. Rose hugged Mora tightly. "This is unexpected." Mora said with concern. "I just got notification about what happened to your school today, why didn't you tell me about this?" asked Dr. Rose. "Mom, I am ok really; we were saved by a bunch of super heroes today so everyone was saved." reassured Mora. "I'm just glad you're ok!" Dr. Rose said with care. "We were saved by a new hero too, a female superhero, of course there were three other heroes too, but she was really cool." said Mora. "Really? What was her name?" asked Dr. Rose. "Umm...She never said." answered Mora. Mora realized she never gave her hero a name, she thought about it and wondered what her superhero name could be. She guesses that would have to wait for later, for she was in the middle of a conversation with her mother. Mora grabbed a banana, and Dr. Rose turned on the TV to watch the news.

The TV showed the news where it was talking about the Blaster incident at the school today, all of the sudden Mora gets a phone call. When she said hello to the caller, it turned out to be none other than Albert Zand. Mora almost choked on her banana, because she knew whatever this was it had to be big! "You ok sweetie?" asked Dr. Rose. "Yeah, it's just Jessie talking to me, he told me a funny joke and that's why I choked." answered Mora. "Anyways I should probably take this call, bye." said Mora. Mora ran up to her room, and locked the door to make sure her mother wouldn't hear her talking to Albert Zand. "How did you get my number?" asked Mora. "We're Zand, we know everything." answered Albert. "So, you know who I am?" asked Mora. "It's ok kid, your secret is safe with us." answered Albert. "Anyways the reason why I called you this evening is to let you know that we've a special mission for you if you're willing to help us." said Albert. Mora couldn't believe what she was hearing; and was beyond excited. She jumped in the air with her hand up with joy after hearing that Zand needs her help.

Mora told Albert that she is down for the mission, after the call ended, she uses her powers to transform into her superhero persona. She took off in the night sky to head to Albert Zand, Albert texted her his location, which is at the public cemetery in Hillsview. Mora arrives at the public cemetery to see a bunch of security guards, and people from Zand everywhere. She then notices something else; she sees the grave of Valiant one of Earth's strongest heroes. His grave looked like he was robbed, Albert walked up to Mora to give Mora the scoop on what is going on. Albert says that a group of Russian super villains have taken the body of Valiant and are planning to take the body to Russia to create an army of Valliant's to create the ultimate soldiers. "How do you know that?" asked Mora. Albert explained that for years Zand has had secret robot birds with security cameras for eyes that watch over everything, there's nothing they don't see. One of the robot birds from Zand caught footage of the villains taking the body of Valiant from his grave.

Mora was both impressed and shocked. Impressed at the technology that Zand possesses, but also shocked at what just happened. Like villains from Russia just dug up a dead body and took it away from its grave. Mora asks why Russian villains would go after Valiant? Albert Zand explained that for years, Zand and Russia have been at war with each other. Russia always tried to infiltrate our knowledge and use our knowledge against us. Now they're planning to use Valiant's body to make clones of Valiant and create an army of Valiant clone soldiers, to be the ultimate army. Albert tells Mora if they manage to clone

Valiant who knows what could happen, they could declare World War 3 and decide to overrule the whole world. Mora knew that this was serious, but she was down for the mission. "I won't let you down, Mr. Zand!" swore Mora. A Zand agent walks up to Albert saying that thanks to the tracker that they placed on Valiant's body they infiltrated the body's location, it's on a train headed to Russia.

Albert tells Mora that she must find the train and retrieve the body. Mora agreed and heads out there to find the train. Zand puts a tracker watch on her to track her every move so that they know she is doing the job and is safe. Zand sends her the coordinates to the trains and she flies very far to find the train. While she is flying, she receives a FaceTime call from her mom. Mora freaks out because she doesn't know what to do, plus it's like ten o clock at nighttime. She is getting worried because what if she came to check up on Mora in her room to see if she was asleep or not? Mora declined the call; she is flipping out because she doesn't know what to do. She then is receiving a phone call from her mother, along with a text that says, "Answer me!" Mora knew she couldn't just ignore her mother, so she answered the phone. "Hello." Mora nervously greeted.

"Where are you?!" Dr. Rose exclaimed with concern. "I'm uh...asleep." Mora answered with an unconvincing fib. "I'm in your room, don't lie to me!" shouted Dr. Rose. "This is not alright, now where are you really?!" Dr. Rose asked demanding an answer. Mora was terrified to answer, but she knew she had to tell her the truth. Mora took a deep breath, inhaled powerfully, and began to speak. "I'm in the sky." answered Mora. "What do you mean the sky?!" asked Dr. Rose. Before Mora could explain more Dr. Rose talked over her. "What have we talked about you using your powers outside, what if someone sees you?", "Somebody has already seen me...I'm on a mission right now...doing a sort of a superhero thing." Mora cut in with an anxious explanation. For thirty seconds there was no answer, this made Mora nervous for she really wanted to hear something, just anything really. "Mom, can you please say something?" Mora anxiously asked with a tear drop from her eye falling.

Mora hears an angry sigh coming from Dr. Rose's voice coming from her phone, she knew she was not happy. "I want you to come home to the house right now!" demanded Dr. Rose. "Well...I can't really do that." said Mora. "What?! Why?!" asked Dr. Rose. Mora explains to Dr. Rose that she is working for Zand on a mission to stop some Russians from cloning Valiant for their evil purposes. Dr. Rose was shocked when she heard the name Zand, she knew they would come back for Mora. "Mora, listen to me! You don't know Albert Zand like I do, he's a very dangerous person!" warned Dr. Rose. "Oh, like you know him personally." Mora said mockingly. Dr. Rose kept trying to warn her more, but Mora wouldn't listen for she felt like her mother was holding her back from a great opportunity. So, she decided to not listen. Dr. Rose commanded her to come back home, but Mora rudely refused. "No! I'm not listening to you!" exclaimed Mora. "I have an opportunity to become a real superhero, and I'm not letting you take this away from me!" Mora exclaimed again.

"You don't understand...", "No you don't understand!" interrupted Mora. "You've kept me, the real me hidden almost my whole life! Nobody knows the real me! I'm seventeen years old, and no one knows who I truly am. The reason why I want to become a superhero is to just be me." explained Mora. Mora furiously wiped all the tears coming from her eyes, as she angrily told her mother all the stuff that she has been keeping inside for a long time. "I'm doing this mission. I'll finally become a part of Zand, and I'll get to live a much better life, you'll see." said Mora. Mora looks at her phone to see that her target is moving farther away and figures she should continue her mission than just sitting in one place talking to her mom. "I got to go mom." said Mora. Dr. Rose begged her not to hang up, but she did anyways. Dr. Rose was so angry that she threw her phone across the way cracking the screen. Mora then continued her mission to find the Russian train to retrieve the body.

Dr. Rose knew that she had to do something, she wasn't sure what she was going to do but she knew she had to do something to save her daughter. She got her keys and planned to head to the car. When she opened the door, she saw Albert Zand along with a bunch of Zand bodyguards. "Deja fucking Vu, right?" Albert Zand asked rhetorically. Meanwhile we see Mora finally make it to Russia, where we see snowy mountains and gray skies. Mora was flying over the train that was carrying the body. Mora stopped right in the middle of the train tracks waiting for the train to come, the train tried to stop once a Russian conductor saw a little girl in the middle of the tracks. Mora uses her powers to change the train tracks from metal to a melting sticky substance, stopping the train literally in its tracks before it could hit her. So, after the train was stopped, she began entering all the cars on the train to find where the body was located. A couple of the cars she traveled just had guards on them that she had to fight, and she took care of them without breaking a sweat.

After fighting cars of Russian guards, she eventually goes to the car that had the body. To Mora's surprise, it appeared that Valiant's dead body has been torn apart, which is shocking because Valiant is known to be invulnerable. So how could the Russians cut him up into pieces? It also looked like some of his organs were missing. Mora also saw a containment cube of water with a young man inside, she figured that this must be their clone. Mora contacts Albert Zand through the tracker all he gave her, to tell him what's up. She tells him that the body is destroyed but sees that they just made their first clone. It also looks like they duplicated the clone by placing his organs into a new body which is this clone and is going to use this clone to clone more clones. Albert tells Mora to grab the clone and get out of there. Mora uses her powers to turn the electricity into liquid, malfunctioning the system of the tube that the clone is in. Then the tube unloads the water along with the clone. She looks at the clone, to notice how sweet and innocent the clone of the most powerful hero on the planet looks.

Mora touches the right side of the face of the clone feeling what it's like to touch a clone. The clone wakes up, starts speaking in a gibberish language, Mora figures that this Clone was just created so it probably doesn't have any knowledge of how to speak. "Hey it's ok. I'm here to get you out of here. I promise you're safe with me." reassured Mora. As Mora picked up the clone, all of a sudden a red blur takes the clone out of Mora's hands. She turns out to see a bunch of costume people right behind her. She figures that this must be the Russian villains that Albert was telling her about. "So, you're the villains who stole Valiant's body and decided to make a mini version of him." observed Mora. A man with a long brown beard walks up saying, "Villains? We're not villains."; "And I'm pretty sure that's not a Russian accent." said Mora. "Who are you guys?" asked Mora. "I'm glad you asked." answered the long bearded man. Next all the other costume people behind walk forward revealing themselves from beyond the shadows they hid behind.

"We're the Redeemers of Russia!" introduced the long bearded man. "My name is Samson. I'm very strong!" The long bearded man introduced himself by revealing his real name. "This is Thunder Woman, Red Bullet, Crowbar, and Vigilante-X." Samson introduced the other Russian heroes. To Mora they just looked like a Russian knock off of the United. "Look it's been fun hanging out with you wanna be's, but I got to return this to Zand so I'll catch you chumps on the flip side." Red Bullet zooms his way towards Mora taking the clone's body away from her. "The boy stays with us!" exclaimed Red Bullet. Mora knew if she was going to get the clone, she was going to have to fight her way through this. "Ok which one of you assholes wants their ass beaten first?" Mora asked rhetorically. Tensions rose between the team of Russian heroes and Mora. Mora's eyes turned pink, Thunder Woman's eyes turned electric blue, Crowbar got his crowbar out, Vigilante-X got in his combat stance, Red Bullet was getting ready to make a run, and finally Samson pulled a big axe from his back. Both sides were ready for a brawl.

The Redeemers run to Mora, while Mora flies at intense speed towards the Redeemers. Mora takes on Samson, Samson tries to chop her with his axe. She dodged the attack, giving him a punch to his chin. You see both Thunder Woman flying towards Mora, and Red Bullet running at super speed towards Mora. Thunder Woman was going to release a Thunder punch to her, and Red Bullet was going to release a super speed punch at the same time to make a super powered combo move. To their surprise Mora grabs the two heroes by the back of the head, and slams both of their heads together making them butt heads. The battle has already begun, and she's already taken down three heroes, suddenly she gets kicked in the face by Vigilante-X. Mora noticed a drop of blood from her nose, she couldn't believe that she was bleeding from an attack from a man who just looks like a regular mortal. "How?" asked Mora. "Ever since my time in the Russian Army, their scientists gifted me with a serum that gives me super strength, and agility. Which makes me strong enough to even put holes through walls!" Vigilante-X explained.

He then punched her again; Mora then blasted him using her atom blast out of the palm of her hands. Suddenly a crowbar hits her in the back of the head, not really physically affecting her. Crowbar noticed that didn't do much damage, she turns around to see him. "I'm so sorry." apologized Crowbar. Red Bullet runs towards Mora tackling her to the wall, then he used his super speed to punch and kick Mora continuously. Flows of blood came from her mouth, and her nose. "Not too unbreakable now, are you?!" insulted Red Bullet. Thunder Woman uses her electricity powers to lift Mora off the ground, Mora screams in pain as she feels the electricity going through her body. Thunder Woman uses her electric powers to slam Mora to both the left and right wall continuously. Samson then stops the wall slamming, by hitting Mora in the back making her slam drop to the ground with blood bursting from her mouth as she slowly jumped from the ground to up in the air.

Mora drops back to the ground, with puddles of her blood surrounding her. Her eyes wide open, even red too. Mora tries to catch her breath but it's hard for she feels like her lungs have been damaged. She can breathe, just not hardly. Vigilante-X kicks her in the stomach just to knock some more blood out of her body. "That's enough!" Samson said to Vigilante-X. "She is taken care of, we're victorious and now the clone belongs to us." said Samson. "Someone put that thing back in its tube!" commanded Vigilante-X. Crowbar tries to pick up the clone, the clone's eyes suddenly began to turn red. The clone's eyes then blasted heat vision; the clone tried shutting off his eyes by closing them, but it just ended up hurting him. He began blasting his heat vision everywhere, he accidentally used his heat vision to burn off the left arm of Crowbar. "Fuck!" painfully screamed Crowbar. His heat vision continued to go all over the place, the Redeemers took cover and tried to avoid getting blasted. "Somebody stop him!" commanded Vigilante-X.

The whole time this was going on Mora was still on the ground just trying to catch her breath, while coughing up drops of blood from her mouth. She sees Thunder Woman charging up to throw a punch at the clone, Mora knew she had to do something. We see Thunder Woman charging up electricity in her right fist getting prepare for a knockout punch strong enough to knock him out. Mora thought of something, and hoped it would work, she used her atom manipulating abilities to change Thunder Woman's right fist into the size of a toddler's fist. Making the punch not being able to physically hurt him, which also left Thunder Woman with a broken baby fist leaving her screaming in pain just like Vigilante-X. Mora slowly got up, with her two arms lifting her body and her using her shaking feet to regain balance. The clone then falls unconscious after his heat vision let up. Mora quickly flies and grabs the clone before he could even touch the ground. Mora was carrying the clone into the night air, heading back to Hillsview to give Albert Zand his clone.

Mora contacted Albert telling him that he had the clone. "Excellent! I'm sending the coordinates to you now to bring the clone to us, we'll be waiting." said Albert. As Mora was flying with the unconscious clone in her arms, she was having painful flashbacks of the beating she just got from the Redeemers. She remembers just feeling completely weak, remembering what Red Bullet said, and just watching herself get destroyed like that. To her it felt like she was literally about to die, which scared her because she thought she was going to die without getting her shot, or without telling her mom how much she loved her. It left her breathing hard and left her heart pumping excessively as well. Was this PTSD? Was she having a panic attack? She didn't know, so she stopped at a spot on a mountain for a minute, just to catch her breath. She knew that heroes had to go through this type of stuff, but she thought she would be fine. She didn't feel fine, she felt terrified. Like she just met the devil for the first time or something.

Eventually she was able to calm herself down, so she continued to finish her mission, and deliver the clone to Albert. She makes it to Hillsview about an hour later, but as she follows the coordinates to Albert Zand something began to not seem right. She was close to his location, but his location seems to be in her neighborhood. Things were then getting suspicious, then the coordinates were revealed to be at Mora's house which concerned her. She did not know what to expect next, she slowly opened the door to her house walking with the clone in her arms. "Hello?" called out Mora. Suddenly the lights turned on revealing several Zand guards, and Albert Zand with a gun pointed at the head of a tied up Dr. Rose. Mora saw the gun, and got angry, and worried at the same time. Mora set the body down, lifted up giving Albert Zand an angry face. "You sure you want to do that?" ask Albert Zand. Mora calmed down and dropped herself back to the ground with her hands up. "I brought you your clone, so why are you doing this?" asked Mora.

"You." answered Albert Zand. Mora was confused about what he meant. Albert then explains everything to Mora about how she is actually a property of Zand, how she actually should've been a hero earlier in life. They explained that for years Zand made money off superheroes in order for them to thrive. Albert knew that everyone loved superheroes, so he gave the world heroes that little boys and girls can look up to. Did that mean kidnapping kids, and forcing them into a life they didn't want to be? Yes, Albert has been doing this superhuman kid's trafficking thing for years, ever since the nineties. Albert also explains to Mora that Dr. Rose is not her biological mother, she took Mora away from Zand because she feared about the life that Mora would get if she stayed with Zand. Albert said they came not only to retrieve the clone, but to also get something that belonged to them from the get go. Albert's plan was to tell the world that they now have new heroes to become part of the next generation of the United, Mora and the clone would be the new heroes; and the new face of Zand.

Albert tried to convince Mora to join by saying how much good she would do, how much money they would make off her, and how famous she would be. Mora thought about it too, but by looking at her mom's face she knew that's not what her mother would've wanted. She also knew that real heroes don't do it for fame, fortune, or status. They do it for the betterment of mankind, and the improvement of life all around. "What do you say, kid? You want to come home, back where you truly belong?" Mora looked at Albert's face and says, "Fuck you!" While also spitting on the right cheek of his face, the Zand guards pointed their guns at Mora with lasers pointing all over her body. "You're going to regret doing that!" Shouted Albert. He slaps her, but his slap has zero effect on her. "After everything, after all the opportunities I've given you, this is how you repay my kindness?!" Albert shouted once more with fury.

Albert told the guards to fire their weapons, but before the bullets could even touch Mora, she turned the powder into rustic dust. Mora looks back at Albert punches at him, but her punch phases through him. Revealing that Albert Zand this whole time was just a hologram. "You coward! You don't have the actual guts to face me!" yelled Mora. "I'm smart, not stupid." replied Albert. Albert also reveals that her mother in the living room is also a hologram, and they have her at Zand. He said she has been rehired and is going to help us once again. Albert says he is giving Mora twenty-four hours to reconsider her offer. If she doesn't make up her mind her mother will die, and they'll report Mora for grave robbing. For they edited the video to make it seem as if she dug up the grave of Valiant and stole his body. So now Mora must make a choice to either join Zand or go against a company that can ruin her life. The guards took the clone and warned her what will happen to the clone if she follows them. She didn't want anything bad to happen to the clone, so she respected their threat.

After the guards left with the clone, Mora was then all alone. She became mad, furious that Zand tricked her. This whole time she thought this was a chance for her to prove herself that she could be something she always wanted to be, but it all turned out to be a lie. She knew despite all the dishonesty and betrayal she must save her mom from Zand. She began to worry about her mother, because she thought to herself about the possibility of this being the last time she ever saw her mother alive again. Even though she lied to Mora her whole life, and even though she is not Mora's biological mother. For years she was a mother to Mora, so she must set course to Zand industries to rescue her mom. She didn't think she can do this alone either, so she knew she was going to need some help and she knew exactly who to call for help. She thought of the heroes she met along the way like Blue Bird, Scarlet Tiger, Rubber Girl, and Moonlight. She thought they would make the perfect team to help her.

Mora took flight to the city of Hillsview, where she eventually finds the crime fighting duo Scarlet Tiger and Rubber Girl on patrol eating snacks. Scarlet Tiger offered Rubber Girl a bite of her Peanut Butty Buddy. "Eww! You know I'm allergic to nuts." informed Rubber Girl. Mora slowly flies behind them saying hi, the two heroes were frightened for they didn't know someone was behind them. "I know you! You're that girl we fought crime with at that school against the Blaster." said Scarlet Tiger. "Why are you here?" asked Rubber Girl. Mora explained to the crime fighting duo the whole thing about Zand with them, and what they're up to. "So, this whole time superheroes we looked up to were trafficked into this life?" asked Rubber Girl. Mora shook her head saying yes to her question. "That's fucked up!" exclaimed Scarlet Tiger. "I know that's why we need to hand together to stop them before they can do this to anyone else." said Mora.

"And why should we help you?" asked Rubber Girl. "I don't know, because you guys are heroes just like me and you want to do the right thing." answered Mora. "Look I don't expect you to believe me I couldn't believe it either. All I know is there is somebody out there that I care about that is about to enter a life of pain if we don't stop Zand. They also have my mom. I don't know if you guys have moms, but I love mine very dearly. She means the world to me, and if anything happened to her, I wouldn't be able to forgive myself." said Mora. "I just ask that you fight with me to save the kid and save my mom." pleaded Mora. Scarlet Tiger and Rubber Girl looked at each other unsure about this, but they thought to each other that this is something they should do. "Ok we're in." said both Scarlet Tiger and Rubber Girl. "Thank you!" said Mora. "Now we just need to find some other heroes to want to fight Zand with us." said Mora. "Do any of you two know where I can find Moonlight, or Blue Bird?" asked Mora. The two crime fighting duo smile at Mora to give her a hint that they do know where to find them.

Mora and the crime fighting duo set out on the town to find Blue Bird and Moonlight. Rubber Girl using her stretching powers to create long legs to travel, Scarlet Tiger rode on Mora's back just for fun. "So, you gotta name?" asked Scarlet Tiger. "My name is Mora." answered Mora. "No, no, no, I mean do you have a superhero name?" asked Scarlet Tiger. Mora gulped because she didn't even think what her superhero name should be, so she humorously lied and said, "Of course I do it's uhh...it's umm.." "You don't have one, do you?" asked Scarlet Tiger. "No, I don't." Mora answered truthfully. "That's ok it took a little bit for us to come up with nicknames too, well more her than me but whatever." reassured Scarlet Tiger. "What's your powers?" asked Rubber Girl. "I can manipulate atoms." answered Mora. "Anything else?" asked Rubber Girl. "I can fly, I have super strength, and invulnerability." answered Mora. "Well, there you go, do something with invulnerability." suggested Rubber Girl.

Mora didn't think that was a bad idea, because she always felt a sense of invulnerability with her powers, and within herself. Suddenly Rubber Girl says, "We're here!" "Where's here?" asked Mora. The three heroes were on top of an apartment building. "This is where the Blue Bird lives." answered Rubber Girl. "How do you know where he lives?" asked Mora. "We put an Air Tag on him, so we can track him on our phones." answered Scarlet Tiger. "You did what?!" Mora asked with shock. "Relax you said you need a team, right? Well, this is our next team member so let's get his ass and get this show on the road." said Scarlet Tiger. The three heroes enter the apartment, where we see hot mist coming from the open bathroom door. They see him taking a shower, listening to a song by Childish Gambino called "3005". Scarlet Tiger hands

Rubber Girl her phone saying, "Record this shit." Scarlet Tiger sneaks into the shower with the Blue Bird singing with him, he notices someone else's voice in the shower with him. He sees Scarlet Tiger, jumps in fear knocking him out of the shower.

"The hell you are doing in my apartment?!" asked Blue Bird. Scarlet Tiger laughs coming out of the shower. "Y'all aren't going to be laughing once I kick all your asses!" threatened Blue Bird. "Now who sent you?" asked Blue Bird. "Nobody...We need your help." answered Mora. After Blue Bird got some clothes on, Mora explains to Blue Bird about the whole thing with Zand just like how she did with Scarlet Tiger and Rubber Girl. "I don't believe that." said Blue Bird. "Y'all honestly expect me that the CEO of Zand is a hungry money monster making a buck off of superhuman kids by trafficking them into a lifestyle they didn't even want in the first place?" asked Blue Bird. "We were hoping you did." answered Scarlet Tiger. Rubber Girl bumped her shoulder for that was not the right thing to say at the time. Mora tried to convince him that what she was saying was true, but Blue Bird still wasn't convinced. Mora couldn't convince him anymore, so she said, "You don't have to come with us, but that's the truth."

"Come on guys, let's find Moonlight." Mora said to Rubber Girl and Scarlet Tiger as they left Blue Bird's apartment. Blue Bird thought about her offer and decided to reconsider and help the girls out. "Do you guys have an air tag on Moonlight?" asked Mora. "Unfortunately, we do not." answered Rubber Girl. "Then how are we going to find Moonlight?" asked Mora. "I can take you to him." Blue Bird answered dangling on the rooftop beside Mora, Scarlet Tiger, and Rubber Girl. "Yay! So, you're going to help us?" asked Scarlet Tiger. "All I'm saying is this better not be some sick joke like sneaking into my shower was, but if you guys are telling the truth then yes, I'll help." answered Blue Bird. Scarlet Tiger and Rubber Girl cheered with excitement now that Blue Bird has joined them, Mora gives Blue Bird a smile to show her appreciation for his reconsideration. So Mora, Scarlet Tiger, Rubber Girl, and Blue Bird are on the move to find Moonlight.

Mora, Scarlet Tiger, and Rubber Girl travel the same way they did when they were trying to find Blue Bird. Blue Bird traveled on his Bird Cycle, which was a motorcycle that was Blue Bird themed. "You have a motorcycle?! Awesome!" Scarlet Tiger said gleefully. "So where can we find Moonlight?" asked Mora as they flew to their unknown location. "Where they always are." answered Blue Bird. The group of heroes see Moonlight on top of a gargoyle looking down on Hillsview. "This city sleeps for now, until the screams of terror wake this sleepy city." said Moonlight talking to themself. "That's why I'm here to silence those who dare to wake my city with their treacherous acts. There is no one like me, there is no one who will go to lengths for this city just like me, like these other heroes in this city will." said Moonlight. "You know we can hear you right?" asked Rubber Girl. Moonlight turns around and asks, "What are you doing here?"

Mora got tired of explaining, but she knew she had to tell them everything again! While Mora was explaining, some of the heroes noticed that Moonlight looked different. More feminine than usual. "Did you get a new suit?" asked Rubber Girl. "Don't worry about it." Moonlight rudely answered. Moonlight tells them that a being he talks to named Lunak senses that what they're saying is true. For Moonlight's last host also experienced the torture that Zand gave to him and his fellow teammates in the United. "Host?" asked Blue Bird. "Long story short the reason why Moonlight has been around for a long time is because of different host taking on the role of

Moonlight." explained Moonlight. Everyone looked at him weirdly, because of their confusion of what Moonlight was saying. "What? You think one person was Moonlight the whole time? What do you think Moonlight is immortal?" Moonlight asked with sarcasm. "Yes." answered Mora, Blue Bird, Scarlet Tiger, and Rubber Girl.

"So, are you going to help us?" asked Mora. "Sure, the city is sleeping well tonight. So why not save the world by saving superhuman kids." answered Moonlight. Mora was happy now that she finally had a team to help her save the kid, and her mom. So, the team set forward to Zand industries, with the time being eight a.m. It's been a long night for Mora, but she must continue further. Mora and her team of fellow heroes made it to Zand Industries, showing up to the entrance. They made an entrance walking in, for Mora used her atom blast to create a giant blast to let Albert Zand know that they're here. The lady at the front desk panics and pushes a button to alert the Zand guards of an intruder alert. The guards showing up demanding for the intruding heroes to get down and put their hands in the air. The heroes did not obey their command and decided to stand tall.

The heroes clashed against the Zand guards, defeating anyone that came across their paths. After five minutes of fighting ten guards in one lobby, they finally defeated them thanks to their powers and skills. Rubber Girl saw the desk lady making a run for it, but she stopped her by wrapping her with her stretchy long left arm. She used her stretchy left arm to wrap her like a blanket, then twirled her back to her direction. Moonlight's feminine suit, changes to his regular masculine suit as he approaches the desk lady. Moonlight takes the desk lady and uses their arm to hold her neck against the wall. "Where is your boss? Tell us now!" demanded Moonlight. "Moonlight, that's enough!" Mora exclaimed. "Not until she gives us answer." said Moonlight. "Where is Albert Zand?" asked Moonlight. "I can't tell you that." answered the desk lady. "Ok then..." said Moonlight. Moonlight took a rod from their rod holder compartment and used it to press against the desk lady's neck causing her to choke.

Moonlight lifted his rod up, along with her body which caused her choking to become excessive. Mora and the others couldn't believe their eyes at what Moonlight was doing. "Now I'm going to ask again...Where is Albert Zand?" asked Moonlight as he kept pressing up his rod to the desk lady's chin. "In the lab...In the forest...He's holding kids there." the desk lady answered with every breath she had left. Moonlight spared her by dropping her, the desk lady began grasping for air while feeling her neck again after that painful interrogation. "We now know where he is, so let's go." Moonlight told the others as he walked out of the building. "That was uncalled for." Mora said to Moonlight. "We needed answers, and we got them. That's what matters." replied Moonlight. So, the team took off from the forest to find the lab, to stop their big operation. The team finally finds the lab, looking bigger than ever. They had big, armored cars driving up the lab, superhuman kids lined up, guards everywhere in case something goes down.

We see our courageous heroes hiding behind the bushes, thinking what their next plan should be. "We need a plan." said Blue Bird. "I say we go in there and fuck shit up!" suggested Scarlet Tiger. "No, we need a real plan." said Mora. "I got one." said Moonlight. "Blue Bird and I will stop those trucks from taking those kids, Rubber Girl and Scarlet Tiger clear the way for Mora to get inside so she can save her mom." explained Moonlight. "How about the snipers watching out for intruders?" asked Blue Bird. Moonlight sighed with exhaustion and said, "Fine! I'll take care of the snipers. Blue Bird will deal with the guards and the trucks." "So, you just expect me to do take out an army of guards, and save all these kids by myself?" asked Blue Bird. "Yes." answered Moonlight. "Sounds good enough, let's get a move on!" exclaimed Rubber Girl. Rubber Girl, Scarlet Tiger, and Moonlight were headed to their tasks. Blue Bird was about to do his task, but he notices that Mora is nowhere to be found.

Blue Bird hears a gasp for air, like someone is hyperventilating. He hears it behind the bushes, he opens the bushes to see Mora trying to catch her breath. Mora's eyes were wide open, sweat drops dropped from her forehead, and her legs were shaking. She couldn't help but remember the last time she was a hero. When the Redeemers of Russia were beating her senseless, it's like she was reliving it all over again. She could even remember the pain she felt. From the pain of Samson's axe hitting her back with his mighty axe, from Thunder Woman's Thunder powers leaving a shock to her nerves, and Red Bullet speed punching and kicking the mess out of her. She was nervous of what would be in store for her, she was also scared for her mother's life for one bad move and Albert might kill her. Mora was panicking, and worried. Tears began to come to the surface of her eyes as if she never felt so much fear in her life. Blue Bird tapped her shoulder asking if she was ok, she turned around in surprise for she didn't know Blue Bird was right there.

"Yeah, I'm ok I just needed some air." answered Mora. "Are you sure? Because it looked like you were having a panic attack." Blue Bird asked again. Mora slammed her eyes shut and said, "I can't do this!" Blue Bird asks why she can't do this, she tells him the reason out of fear. She fears after her almost death incident a few hours ago with the Redeemers that what if it happens again? She was also afraid for her mother; she didn't want anything bad to happen to her mother. "Blue Bird took her hand and said this, "Your mom is going to be ok; we'll save her." "How do you know?" asked Mora. "Because I believe in you!" answered Blue Bird. "I know you may doubt yourself, but just know that even when you're breakable you can also be unbreakable! I know you're scared to put yourself out there again after that traumatizing battle with the Redeemers, but you've got to bring yourself to the now. You're still alive and that's what makes you unbreakable. It shows me how much of a punch you can truly take." said Blue Bird.

Mora took Blue Bird's words and took them as like faith. She suddenly felt this sense of empowerment, this invulnerability. She floated up, opening her eyes with her eyes glowing pink. "Let's go save the world." said Mora. Blue Bird smiled at Mora's comeback to see her ready to help fight Albert Zand and put an end to his evil deeds. Mora and Blue Bird run to the others to fulfill their tasks as planned. "You know that could be your name." Blue Bird said with a suggestion. "What could be my name?" asked Mora. "Unbreakable or something with Unbreakable in it." answered Blue Bird. As Mora and Blue Bird traveled to their destinations, she thought of what he said, she liked what he said about what her name could be. Eventually Blue Bird went West to the kids, Mora just flew over to where Rubber Girl and Scarlet Tiger were which was the front entrance of the facility. "Took you long enough." scoffed Scarlet Tiger. A guard sees them from the right corner of the entrance, he gets his gun ready to fire.

Moonlight sneaks up behind the guard, puts him in a choke hold with his rod. Brings him down to the ground, then uses his rod to beat the guard. "Move your asses!" Moonlight shouted to Mora, Scarlet Tiger, and Rubber Girl. Moonlight pushes the button on a control panel to open the door for them. Mora, Scarlet Tiger, and Rubber Girl were surprised to see an army of guards in their sights. Mora, Scarlet Tiger, and Rubber Girl got in their fight stances ready for battle. The girls charged with a battle cry as they head out for battle to fight the guards. Meanwhile, the guards outside of the facility were loading up kids into the trucks, all the sudden Blue Bird swoops down slowly using his cape to take down one of the guards. The rest of the guards saw him and began opening fire on him, thankfully Blue Bird got behind one of their armored cars for protection against their bullets. Eventually he traveled to the other side to sneak attack them using his martial arts skills and gadgets to help his fight against the guards.

We turn back to the girls as we see them fighting the guards. Scarlet Tiger slicing up their guns, and then slicing them leaving bloody scars on their bodies. Rubber Girl uses her stretching powers to create a long arm to take down a bunch of guards by swinging them across the wall. Mora was busy trying to get inside, so she used her atom blast to blast through the door. A guard aimed his gun at her, a bullet flies heading for the back of Mora's head. In a shocking speeding minute Rubber Girl used her stretching powers to catch the bullet before it could even touch the back of Mora's head. Mora turns around surprised at seeing Rubber Girl's hand catching the bullet before it could even touch her. "Go! We got this!" Rubber Girl reassured Mora. Mora then flew in the building and began her search for either Albert Zand or her mother. Mora looked everywhere below, eventually she went upstairs to check if she could find what she was looking for.

She looks up a room upstairs and sees her mother tied up in a chair. Mora flies to the room she is in by breaking into the glass window to enter the room. Mora hugged her mom very tightly, as she almost cried seeing her mother for she feared that she would never see her again. "I'm so glad you're ok." Mora sighed with joy. Mora used her powers to untangle the ropes that her mother was tied in. "We need to get out of here now!" exclaimed Dr. Rose. "Yes, we will as soon as we save the kids..." Mora was interrupted with a strong punch to her face. That punch came from Albert Zand. "Mora!" cries Dr. Rose. Mora gets up with a red cheek on her face after she just got punched. "How did you..." Before Mora could ask, Albert answered by saying, "I stole some powers from one of the kids we studied on, including the clone." Mora's eyes opened with rage as she heard about the clone for she feared what happened to him.

"What did you do to him?!" Mora shouted with a question. "Let's just say that superhuman kids don't last long once their superpowers have been drained from their body." Albert Zand answered with an evil smile. Mora gritted her teeth as she came to the realization that he killed the clone and God who knows how many other kids he killed to get those powers. "You'll pay for what you've done!" Mora cried as she flew to him, bringing him to the wall. Albert Zand's strength was on the same level as Mora's so he was able to go head to head with her. Mora was about to hit him with an atom punch, but Albert stopped her by placing both his three fingers on her forehead. Suddenly the scenery changed to the Russian train she was on when she was fighting the Redeemers. "Remember this?" asked Vigilante-X as he punched her in the face. It turns out that Albert Zand placed Mora in an illusion to make her live her most terrifying moment, so that's all that Mora could see. Mora tried to snap out of it, but it was hard because that's all she saw.

Mora eventually snapped out of the illusion after taking a few beatings of the imaginary Redeemers. She wakes up, back in the lobby she was in when she was fighting Albert. She sees his eyes glowing red, meaning he was going to blast her with heat vision. Before his heat vision could reach Mora, she used her atom blast to overpower the heat vision. It didn't exactly overpower it all the way, it just protected her from getting roasted too death. While they're blasting each other, we see Blue Bird still fighting the guards fighting for his life. Two guards sneak up behind him tasing him on both side of his lungs, Blue Bird screamed in pain as he felt the shock to his lungs. The guards hovered over him, began kicking him and shocking him with their taser sticks. Blue Bird was soon saved by Moonlight who showed up out of nowhere using his smoke bombs to create a distraction long enough for him to sneak attack on all the guards.

After the smoke cleared Blue Bird sees all the guards knocked out, then he sees Moonlight in their feminine hero suit offering their hand to help pick Blue Bird off the ground. "Let's save these kids." said Moonlight. Moonlight and Blue Bird opened all the doors to the armored cars where the kids were, Blue Bird told them that it was ok for them to come out their safe now. Now back to Mora, we see her being choked by Albert Zand telekinetically, we see her up in the air holding on to her neck as she feels the force of his telekinesis choking her. Albert Zand tells Mora all the powers he has now from all the kids he has drained and killed. He explains the power of his telekinesis, his ability to fly, make people see illusions, shoot heat vision from his eyes, and how he's strong enough to withstand Mora. As Albert was distracted talking, Mora tried hard to use her atom powers to try to make the ceiling crumble that was over Albert's head.

It was difficult for Albert to choke her even harder, which made it difficult for her to focus her powers. "You could've had it all Mora! Fame, fortune, and the best life possible." said Albert. "What's good of that life if you don't have a choice in the matter?" Mora asked while still trying to speak. Albert choked her even harder with his telekinesis, her face was even turning fully red, that's how harder he was getting. "I gave them a good life! They gave me a good life! You could've had that, but you decided to be a coward and hide your light from the world! I could've helped you with that potential, but your poor excuse for a mother took that from you!" shouted Albert. "Now I will have to kill you both!" threatened Albert. Albert uses his telekinesis to grab Dr. Rose by the throat choking her while lifting her off the ground just like Mora. "It's a shame you're going to die and you don't even have a superhero name! Like what kind of superhero doesn't have a name?!" insulted Albert.

Mora's eyes turned bright pink, and she replied to Albert with, "Actually I do!" Then something crazy happened, the entire scene changed into space again like how it did with her the first time on the bus. She used her powers to absorb atoms all around her. She absorbed so many atoms that pink energy began to form all around her body. She kept absorbing, and absorbing, until all of the sudden something changed, her entire body then began to glow bright pink. Albert and Dr. Rose couldn't believe what they were seeing, it's like she was going super nova. Albert could sense that Mora reached max power, once she absorbed the atoms. Mora was free from Albert's telekinetic grasp; Mora began to fly towards Albert faster than the blink of an eye. Albert was then scared of what was about to happen. "Who are you?!" Albert asked in fear. "I'm Unbreakable!" answered Mora. Finally, Mora had found her superhero name that she had been searching for.

Mora opened her mouth wide releasing a gigantic energy blast towards Albert, blasting him all the way down to the Earth. Not knowing where he would be going, all Mora cared about was that her mother was safe, and he is defeated. Albert's telekinesis stopped working for Dr. Rose, so Dr. Rose began to fall from the ground but thankfully her daughter saves her by catching her before she even drops to the floor. Mora slowly transformed back to her regular form, after setting her mother gently down on the ground she gives her a big hug. "Oh mom! I was so worried about you! I thought I would never see you again!" cried Mora. Dr. Rose shushed Mora hugging her back, comforting her as she teared up with joy. "I'm so proud of you, Mora!" cheered Dr. Rose. Dr. Rose tells Mora that she felt bad for keeping her hidden after all these years, but she explains she thought she was doing it for her own safety.

Mora understood why her mother did what she did, she forgave her for hiding her because she knew why. It wasn't for ill intent, only out of love and safety. "We should probably get out of here." said Mora. "Yes, I agree, let's go." Dr. Rose chuckled as she agreed with her daughter. Mora and Dr. Rose Walk back outside to the entrance, the superhuman children were free from the clutches of Zand. Blue Bird said he called the proper authorities to pick up the kids to bring them to a safer environment. Moonlight taps on Mora's shoulder showing her that he has a hard drive of all the footage of what Zand has been doing to the kids for years. "How did you get that?" asked Mora. "When I was knocking out guards above, I snuck into the security room, grabbed as much footage as I can and compiled them into this hard drive." answered Moonlight. "The world needs to know." said Moonlight.

After the authorities picked up all the superhuman children, Mora and her friends still had one more thing to do. Moonlight gave the hard drive to a news station to play to the entire world, and just like that the truth was revealed. Everyone all over the world saw all the horrible things that Zand had been doing for years, after that the world became outraged at Zand. Outraged for supporting such monsters, without Albert Zand around to run Zand, Zand industries shut down. We see Mora showing up at lunch time at the cafeteria to see her friend Jessie eating lunch by himself. Mora walked up to Jessie as he was eating a sandwich. Jessie was happy to see his friend after not seeing her for half the day of school. "Hey, you!" greeted Jessie as he hugged her tightly. "I missed you!" said Jessie. "I missed you too." said Mora. "Why weren't you here earlier?" asked Jessie. "I...Uhh..." Before Mora could answer she heard a loud voice calling her name. She turned to her right to see that it was Hope, she looked very angry.

Hope speed walked her way over to Mora with fury. "Where the fuck were you?" asked Hope. Mora was still trying to come up with an excuse to answer why she wasn't at school earlier. "Uh, hello?!" Hope grunted as she was waiting for an answer. Suddenly Jessie showed up to save her by answering her. "She was sick!" answered Jessie. "Right, Mora?" asked Jessie. "Yeah...I was throwing up really bad this morning I thought I was sick, but I just had a little bug. It came out as soon as I threw up all morning. But rest assured I'm not sick anymore, and before you ask, I'm not contagious either. So yeah, I'm just fine and dandy." answered Mora. "Eew!" said Hope. "Sorry I wasn't here with you to present the assignment." apologized Mora. "It's fine, we both got an A minus, the minus was for you not being here. But we got a good grade anyways." said Hope. "Who is this guy?" Hope asked Mora as she stared at Jessie.

"This is my best friend, Jessie." answered Mora. "And I know your name, Hope Hartley." said Jessie as he put his hand out for a handshake. Hope lightly touched his hand with her two fingers, she didn't know where his hands had been so that's why she did that. "Of course, you know who I am, everyone knows who I am.," said Hope. Hope then turned her focus towards Mora asking if she was going to let her sit with her and her friend. "Of course, you can." said Mora. Hope joined Mora and Jessie for lunch. Together the three teenagers began talking, laughing, and having a good time with each other's company. Mora was glad that the most popular girl in school was her friend, so now she has the best of both worlds. Her best friend and her popular friend. Everything seemed peachy. Suddenly she received a mysterious text message saying, "Meet us at the rooftop of Joe's Convenient Store." She noticed there was a blue bird emoji at the end, meaning that Blue Bird must've sent it.

After Mora's day of school was over, she used her powers to change into her Unbreakable persona and flew to the location that Blue Bird sent. When Mora arrives at the location, she sees Scarlet Tiger slice a champagne bottle that Rubber Girl was holding. This was a celebration of their victory, of their stopping Zand and not to mention saving many lives in the process. Rubber Girl used her powers to hand everyone glasses and fill them with champagne. Mora landed on the rooftop with them to join in all the fun, they all saw Mora and glad she came for all the fun. Everyone began associating with everyone on the rooftop, everyone laughing and having a good time. Mora tells everyone her superhero name saying that her superhero name is Unbreakable . Blue Bird smiled and raised a glass, proud of her for finding her superhero name. "For Unbreakable!" cheered Blue Bird, as the other heroes cheered with him.

We see Moonlight staring down the street patrolling the streets for any criminal activity. "So you're doing your dark and brooding thing again?" Scarlet Tiger asked Moonlight to annoy him. "Piss off." Moonlight replied. As Mora was talking to Rubber Girl, Blue Bird tapped on Mora's shoulder to talk to her. "Hey, there's someone I want you to meet." said Blue Bird. Blue Bird moves to reveal the person he wants Mora to meet, it is an older man in a suit with a mustache. "Hello Unbreakable, my name is Eric Wilson." greeted Eric. "Nice to meet you." Mora said with uncertainty. "I'm friends with Blue Bird here, he has told me so much about you and your magnificent friends. What you guys did about Zand was remarkable." said Eric. "I talked to Blue Bird to ask you, and everyone here if they would like to continue to do remarkable things with me." said Eric. "What kind of remarkable things?" asked Mora.

"Oh, you know saving the world, stopping bad guys, getting fame and glory." answered Eric. "Sounds a lot like Zand." replied Mora. "Yeah, but except we aren't trafficking kids into a forced lifestyle." said Eric. "I like the sound of that." replied Mora. "Will we get paid?" Scarlet Tiger asked, butting into the conversation. Everyone was out with their hands on their face, and sighed with disbelief. They thought it was an inappropriate question to ask at the moment. Eric smiled and said, "Well shit no one said you were going to be working for free." Scarlet Tiger and Rubber Girl both looked at each other holding each other's hands, jumping up and down with excitement. "Yay! Now I don't have to work a crappy job like McDonalds!" cheered Scarlet Tiger. "So do we have a deal, Unbreakable?" Eric asked as he put his hand out for a confirmation handshake. Mora smiled and answered his question with a confirmation handshake. "You got yourself a deal." answered Mora.

Everyone cheered as a grand opportunity was headed their way. Life couldn't get any better for Mora at this moment, but this does not mean her story as Unbreakable is over. For evil still lurks in the shadow of this world. As Mora and her super friends celebrate, we see the green cloaked figure who killed the United on top of a mountain looking down at Hillsview. "Now with Zand out of the way, along with the United we can finally begin our conquest of this planet." the green cloaked figure said to himself. "They won't know what hit them." the green cloaked figure said to himself. The green cloaked figure takes off his hood revealing that the green cloaked figure is none other than the Uranian! Who we all see died, how could this be so? Only time will tell of this great mystery, and what is to unfold is unknown.

Printed in the United States
by Baker & Taylor Publisher Services